Cold Whispers

The SECRET of the TRAGIC THEATER

by Michael Teitelbaum

illustrated by Denise Prowell

BEARPORT
PUBLISHING

New York, New York

Credits

Cover: © Galushko Sergey/Shutterstock, © pryzmat/Shutterstock, and © Skylines/Shutterstock.

Publisher: Kenn Goin
Editorial Director: Natalie Lunis
Creative Director: Spencer Brinker
Text produced by Scout Books & Media Inc.

Library of Congress Cataloging-in-Publication Data

Teitelbaum, Michael.
  The secret of the tragic theater / by Michael Teitelbaum.
      pages cm. — (Cold whispers)
  Summary: A thirteen-year-old girl who likes to sing old songs and dreams of becoming a singing superstar finds herself drawn to an abandoned theater with a tragic past.
  ISBN 978-1-62724-809-9 (library binding) — ISBN 1-62724-809-9 (library binding)
  [1. Singers—Fiction. 2. Ghosts—Fiction.] I. Title.
  PZ7.T233Sg 2016
  [Fic]—dc23
                              2015011898

For more information, write to Bearport Publishing Company, Inc., 45 West 21st Street, Suite 3B, New York, New York 10010.
Printed in the United States of America.

10 9 8 7 6 5 4 3 2 1

Contents

CHAPTER 1
The Audition **4**

CHAPTER 2
A Second Chance? **8**

CHAPTER 3
The Eerie Theater **12**

CHAPTER 4
The Show Must Go On **18**

CHAPTER 5
A Dream Come True **24**

WHAT DO YOU THINK? 30

GLOSSARY 31

ABOUT THE AUTHOR 32

ABOUT THE ILLUSTRATOR 32

CHAPTER 1

The Audition

All her life, everyone who thirteen-year-old Nina Holbrook knew told her she had a beautiful singing voice. Nina had gotten the lead in every school musical—and dreamed of singing on Broadway one day.

More than anything, Nina loved old songs. She even dressed in **vintage** clothes when she sang her favorite oldies. Today, Nina hoped to take a big step on the road to achieving her dream. She was about to audition for the hottest TV talent show on the air—*Singing Superstar!*

On this gray Saturday afternoon, Nina sat in the front seat of her mother's car on her way to the audition.

"You're going to knock 'em dead, as usual, honey," her mother said as they made their way through the city streets.

"This is different, Mom," Nina replied. "It's one thing to be the best singer in *my* school. But all the people who are going to be at this audition are the best in *their* schools, too."

Nina glanced out the window at the bright, blinking **marquee** of the Grand Theater. As they approached, Nina saw a long line of people stretching down the block.

"Oh, man," Nina said. "It looks like everyone in the city is here to audition. Let me out here, Mom."

"Good luck, honey—and don't worry," her mother said as Nina climbed out of the car. "Call me when you're done, all right?"

Nina joined the long line of hopeful singers. She was so far back she could hardly even see the theater. A group of teenage girls stood right in front of her on line. One of the girls, dressed in rainbow-colored pants and a **sequined** shirt, scowled. She looked at Nina's outfit—a vintage 1940s dress—and shook her head.

"What are you dressed up for?" asked the girl. "Halloween is still months away."

"I like vintage clothes," Nina said, smiling. Kids had made fun of her for her **offbeat** taste before. She was kind of used to it. "So what song are you going to audition with?"

"I've practiced a rock song and a rap number," the girl said. "I'll decide last minute once I get a look at the judges. What about you?"

"I'm going to do a song from the 1930s called *Twilight*," Nina said proudly.

"What century are you from?" another girl asked. "They don't pick a winner based on the song the fewest people have heard of, you know."

Nina couldn't wait to get away from these mean girls. When she reached the front of the line, she got a close look at the beautiful theater, all lit up. Her excitement started to build. Then, once inside, it was crushed.

"I'm sorry, miss," said the woman in charge of the line. "We've reached the **maximum** number of singers for this year's contest. You'll have to try again next year."

CHAPTER 2

A Second Chance?

Nina hurried from the theater, staring at the ground, tears streaming down her face.

It's all gone! she thought. *All the hard work, all the practice, all the voice lessons, all for nothing. If I had arrived ten minutes sooner, I'd be up on stage now, singing my heart out, impressing the judges, taking the next step toward—"*

A sudden gust of wind caused Nina to stumble. It sent papers strewn on the street flying through the air in a mini-tornado of trash. As newspapers and food wrappers swirled all around her, Nina lifted her hands to swat away the garbage. A piece of paper smacked her right in the face. As the wind died down, she peeled the page off. She was just about to toss it into a trash can when an image on the paper caught her eye.

Printed on the page was the picture of a beautiful woman on a stage in front of a microphone. She wore a long gown that glittered with sequins. Looking more closely, Nina saw that this was a **flyer** for a performance by a singer named

Dorothy Langford. The paper was yellowed and the image faded. The date of the performance was 1942!

Where did this come from? Nina wondered.

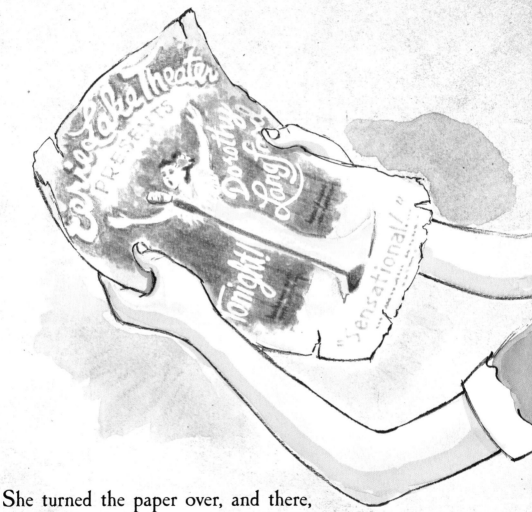

She turned the paper over, and there, on the other side, was a handwritten note that read:

Still want to be a singing superstar? Then come to the Eerie Lake Theater!

"What does this mean?" Nina wondered aloud. "Could this message be for me? And where am I supposed to go?"

Turning the flyer back over, Nina saw an address written in small print and realized that the Eerie Lake Theater was nearby. She looked up at a street sign, then back down at the address on the flyer. Nina was curious, so she headed off toward the address. She completely forgot that she was supposed to call her mother to pick her up.

As she walked, Nina thought about how disappointed she was to have not even gotten a chance to perform at the audition for *Singing Superstar!* At the same time, she was confused by the flyer and note.

A few minutes later, she found herself at the address on the flyer. She stood in front of the Eerie Lake Theater and looked up. All the windows were boarded over. The marquee was shattered in several places and plastic letters dangled from the sign. Broken lightbulbs remained in their **sockets**. Behind a cracked glass display window, a poster showed the same image as the one on the flyer—Dorothy Langford performing in 1942. The building appeared to be totally abandoned.

Nina looked up and down the block. All the other buildings seemed to be abandoned, too. Something darted out in front of her, just inches from her feet. She jumped back, startled, and saw a rat **scurry** into the gutter.

What am I doing here? she thought.

As Nina turned around and pulled out her phone to call her mom, a woman's voice spoke softly from behind her.

"Come in, dear," said the voice. "I've been expecting you. I see you got my note."

CHAPTER 3
The Eerie Theater

Nina spun around, expecting to see someone. No one was there. Then she noticed the front door to the theater was open. She was sure it had been closed a moment ago. She put her phone away and walked toward the door, her heart pounding.

She inched through the open front door. The interior of the theater looked just as run down as the outside—maybe more so. Standing in the lobby, she peeked into the main auditorium, then stepped in. The theater's red velvet seats were **threadbare**. A once-grand chandelier swung **precariously** from the ceiling, its crystals cracked and covered with dust and grime.

Stepping back into the theater's lobby, Nina was overcome by a wave of dizziness. She felt as if the room was spinning. When the spinning stopped, she was confused and amazed by what she saw.

She saw a coat-check room filled with coats, only the styles didn't look modern. Every coat looked as if it had come from one of the old black-and-white movies Nina loved to watch with her grandmother. Women's capes hung from the rack. Men's hats, mostly black **fedoras**, sat neatly on a shelf.

What is happening to me? Nina wondered.

On a wall next to the coatroom, Nina spotted a new-looking poster that read: "Don't forget to buy **War Bonds**. Keep our nation strong!"

War bonds? Nina thought. *I remember learning about them in history class. They sold them during World War II!*

Next to that poster was another that read: "The Spectacular Return of Dorothy Langford—'Queen of the Song' for 1941." Beneath the words was a photo of the beautiful woman in a long, sparkly gown, singing at a microphone. But a banner was pasted across the poster saying: "PERFORMANCE CANCELLED!"

Nina shook her head, squeezed her eyes shut, and took a deep breath. When she opened her eyes, the room was a blur. She grabbed the wall to steady herself. As her focus returned, she saw that the coatroom was now empty and filled with cobwebs. A couple of rusty metal hangers dangled from the bar.

She looked over at the two posters. They were now torn and **tattered**. A yellowed "PERFORMANCE CANCELLED!" banner had fallen to the floor.

The Spectacular Return of Dorothy Langford— 'Queen of the Song' for 1941

PERFORMANCE CANCELLED!

Am I dreaming? Nina wondered. *This can't be real, right?*

Then she remembered the voice that had invited her into the theater. "Hello!" Nina called out **tentatively**. "Is anybody here? Where are you?"

"I'm in my dressing room!" replied the same voice from deep within the theater.

Nina cautiously made her way to the back of the theater. A sudden fluttering sound made her jump. She grabbed a seatback to steady herself. Looking toward the ceiling, she saw a pigeon fly across the theater.

Again the thought came to her: *What am I doing here?* Yet she felt **compelled** to find the strange woman who had invited her in.

Nina slipped backstage and walked slowly down a narrow hallway. Dirty paint peeled from the walls. Overhead, a bare

bulb flickered on and off, making a sizzling sound. Nina felt her heart start to pound again.

Suddenly, a door swung open, its hinges creaking.

Nina peered through the open doorway into a dark room.

"Hello?" Nina called into the darkness.

Light from a floor lamp suddenly **illuminated** a small corner of the room, revealing a woman sitting at a dressing table.

"Come in, dear," said the beautiful woman.

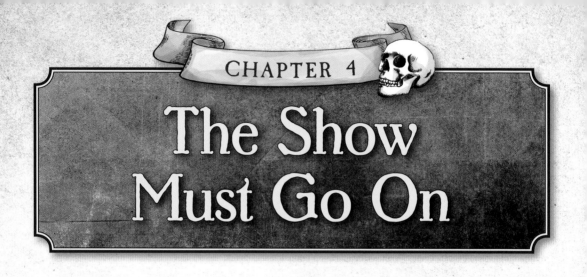

The Show Must Go On

As she stepped into the room, Nina saw a woman surrounded by a shimmering glow. Nina felt as if she could see through her. The woman wore a long gown that was straight out of the 1940s. Her hair was pulled back into an elegant twist topped with a silk flower.

"You have come at last," said the woman, standing up and stepping into a pool of light cast by the lamp.

When the light hit the woman's face, Nina jumped back and gasped.

It's her! The woman from the poster. It's Dorothy Langford! But how can that be? That's impossible!

Before Nina could speak, the woman walked past her and slipped out of the room.

"Follow me, please," she said, gliding down the hallway.

Nina followed, realizing that she could indeed see through

the glowing figure. She was frightened, but still felt as if she had to follow her.

Out of the blue, the dizziness hit Nina again. The backstage area started to spin. This time, when the spinning stopped, Nina found herself standing backstage watching Dorothy Langford prepare to step out onto the stage and sing. The backstage area now looked clean and new, not like it had a few seconds earlier. And Dorothy was no longer surrounded by a glow. Nina could no longer see through her.

Suddenly, Nina heard a terrible cracking noise, then watched in horror as a stage light came crashing down onto Dorothy. Screams of horror rang out backstage as people rushed to Dorothy's side. But they were all too late. Dorothy's lifeless body lay sprawled on the floor.

Nina couldn't believe her eyes. What was she seeing? She squeezed her eyes shut again and counted to ten. When she opened them, Nina was back in the dingy backstage hallway, and the shimmering figure of Dorothy Langford appeared at her side.

"What just happened?" Nina asked, trying to piece together the visions that kept filling her mind. "I just saw you die! You were backstage and a light fell on you. How are you here? What's going on?"

Dorothy looked at Nina longingly. "I—we—are here to complete the performance," she said. Then she walked onto the stage.

"Wh-what do you mean, 'we'?" Nina asked.

All the lights in the theater suddenly went out. Nina stood in total darkness for a few seconds, then a single spotlight flashed on, illuminating the stage in brilliant, blinding light. There, standing in front of a microphone, Nina could make out the glowing figure again.

"Please join me on the stage," Dorothy said to Nina.

Nina stepped onto the stage. She walked toward Dorothy.

Mustering her courage, Nina asked, "Please tell me, how is it possible you're here?"

"You saw my poster," said Dorothy.

"Yes, but that was 1942!" Nina said, trying to make sense of what was happening to her, wondering again if she was dreaming.

"Singing was my life," Dorothy said, sounding sad. "The classic songs of the 1930s were the ones I sang when I first learned how to sing."

"Me too!" Nina said. Finally, this was someone who could understood her love of old songs.

"I know," said Dorothy Langford. "That's why you're here."

Then she spoke into the microphone.

"Ladies and gentlemen," she announced, opening her arms wide. "The singer you've been waiting to hear."

"Ladies and gentlemen"? Nina thought. *There's no one here. The theater is totally empty.*

Nina's thoughts were interrupted by a sudden swell of orchestral music that filled the theater. She looked around. There was no orchestra. Could this be a recording? Then the orchestra played a melody that Nina recognized as one of her favorite old songs. And she was suddenly filled with the desire to sing.

CHAPTER 5

A Dream Come True

Dorothy Langford stepped back and gestured toward the microphone. She handed Nina a piece of sheet music for the song the orchestra was playing.

"No matter what," Dorothy Langford said, "life or death, the show must go on. What has been started must be finished."

Caught up in the emotion of the music and feeling the warmth of the spotlight, Nina stepped up to the microphone. As she opened her mouth to sing, another wave of dizziness came over her and the whole auditorium began to spin. She grasped the microphone stand to keep from falling.

The spinning suddenly stopped, and Nina looked out at a packed house. Every seat in the audience was filled with people dressed in 1940s-style clothing. The theater itself looked new and beautiful, as it must have appeared in its **heyday**.

Nina glanced down and saw that she was now wearing the gown Dorothy Langford had been wearing when she was standing backstage moments earlier. Looking offstage, searching for some answers, Nina caught a glimpse of herself in a mirror.

The face she saw was not her own, but rather the face of Dorothy Langford, as if somehow Nina's thoughts had entered Dorothy's body.

With her mind racing, Nina looked down and saw the orchestra, ready to begin playing. The conductor smiled up at Nina. Then he waved his baton and the orchestra started to play.

Caught up in the emotion and **spectacle**, Nina pushed aside her fear and confusion and sang. She closed her eyes and focused on the song, wringing every drop of emotion from the notes and the **lyrics**.

When she finished, the crowd gave her a standing ovation. Nina smiled and opened her arms wide, as if she wanted to embrace the entire audience. This was her dream come true. She sang as well as she ever had in her life and brought a crowd to its feet.

As Nina looked around, the shimmering, ghostly image of Dorothy Langford appeared next to her on the stage. Dorothy's voice filled Nina's ears. Nina could just make out what Dorothy was saying through the **din** of the cheering crowd.

"In 1942, I was about to step out onto the stage and sing the **finale** of the greatest performance of my career," Dorothy said. "I was about to be crowned 'Queen of the Song' for the second year in a row, assuring my place in music history. But it was not to be.

"My life was tragically cut short by a backstage accident, just before the show's closing number. For decades, my spirit has searched for just the right singer to finish my greatest performance. You made my dream come true, and now I have made yours come true as well.

"I can rest in peace. And you, my dear, have gotten your wish . . . . You are indeed a singing superstar."

The ghostly shimmer faded away as a newspaper reporter carrying a camera came rushing up to the edge of the stage, toward Nina. "It's official. The voting is in. You are 'Queen of the Song' for 1942! Congratulations! How about a picture for the paper?"

A flashbulb went off right in Nina's eyes. Only she was not Nina Holbrook anymore.

"One more photo, Miss Langford, for the *Evening Examiner*," called the photographer.

The Secret of the Tragic Theater

1. How was Nina different from the other kids in line for the *Singing Superstar!* audition?

2. The lobby of the Eerie Lake Theater changes in front of Nina's eyes. Use examples from the story to describe how it changed.

3. Who is shown in the picture at right, and what happens to her in the story?

4. What is happening to Nina in this scene? (bottom picture)

5. If you were in an abandoned theater, would you go onstage and perform? Explain why you would or wouldn't.

compelled (kuhm-PELD) felt a strong desire to take action

din (DIN) a lot of noise

fedoras (fi-dohr-uhz) soft felt hats

finale (fuh-NAL-ee) the last part of a show

flyer (FLYE-ur) a paper handout advertising an event

heyday (HAY-day) a period of great success

illuminated (i-LOO-muh-nay-tid) lit up

lyrics (LIHR-iks) the words of a song

marquee (mar-KEE) a sign above a theater entrance that shows the current play or movie

maximum (MAKS-uh-muhm) the largest amount possible

mustering (MUHSS-tur-ing) gathering or collecting

offbeat (AWF-beet) different from the usual

precariously (pri-KAIR-ee-uhs-lee) unsafely or unsteadily

scurry (SKUH-ree) to move quickly

sequined (SEE-kwind) covered in small shiny disks

sockets (SOK-its) holes where lightbulbs fit

spectacle (SPEK-tuh-kuhl) a magnificent event or sight

tattered (TAT-urd) worn or frayed

tentatively (TEN-tuh-*tiv*-lee) in an unsure manner

threadbare (THRED-bair) worn or shabby

vintage (VIN-tij) old-fashioned

war bonds (WOR BONDZ) investments that helped pay for wars

ABOUT THE AUTHOR

Michael Teitelbaum is the author of more than 150 children's books, including young adult and middle-grade novels, tie-in novelizations, and picture books. His most recent books are *The Very Hungry Zombie: A Parody* and its sequel *The Very Thirsty Vampire: A Parody,* both created with illustrator Jon Apple. Michael and his wife, Sheleigah, live with two talkative cats in a farmhouse (as yet unhaunted) in upstate New York.

ABOUT THE ILLUSTRATOR

Denise Prowell has illustrated several books and many educational materials for children. She lives in northeastern Pennsylvania with her husband, Mark, and has helped to work on a rural and urban land plan in that region. Denise wishes to thank the people of the Scranton Cultural Center, the marvelous theater whose interior was used for visual reference in this book. For these illustrations, Denise used marker, watercolor, acrylic paint, and pastel on watercolor paper.